Wolves

For the earliest reader
by Margaret Hillert

For a very special wolf.
—M.H.

Starfall™
www.starfall.com

Starfall Publications, P.O. Box 359, Boulder, CO 80306

ISBN: 1-59577-037-2

What a pretty spot.

Something will come here.

It is a good spot.

See this.

This is a big, big one.

It can get something good down here.

The baby can get something good, too.

And look at this.

It is so pretty.

This is a good spot for the mother
and the babies.

The big father can do this for
the baby.
The baby will eat and eat and eat.

Some little ones are here, too.
It is fun to play here.
Run, run, run.

Oh, look. A father wolf.

He is big.

He can run and jump.

This is a mother wolf.

She is not so big.

She is pretty.

She can run and jump, too.

The mother and the father
like this spot.

And something little is here, too.
Can you find something here?
One and two and three.

The father will go away.
He wants to find something
to eat.

The mother can give the babies
something to eat.
The babies like it.
It helps the babies get big.

One baby wants to play.

See the baby jump, jump, jump.

That is fun.

This baby wants to run.
No, baby, no.
Run to the mother.

The baby is not here.
Where did it go?
Did it run away?

The mother wants to
find the baby.
She will look and look.

She will look here —

and here —

and here.

Oh, look at this.
Look what is here.
A big, big cat.
This is not good for
the little baby.

The father sees the cat.
He will run at it.
He will make it go away.

The baby is with the father.
This is good.
He will go to the mother now.

Here he is with the mother.
He will not run away.
No, no. He will not run away.

The father is here.

The mother is here.

The babies can play and have fun.

This is a happy, happy spot now.

More Information about Wolves

This book is about the Gray Wolf. As you just read, wolves live together in families. You might have noticed some similarities between the wolf family in this book and your own family, but there are differences, too. A wolf family is called a "pack." Every pack has a mother wolf and a father wolf who are the leaders of the pack. These two are called the "alpha pair." The other wolves in the pack are children and cousins. Packs can have as few as two wolves or as many as 30. Now that's one big extended family!

When it's time for a mother wolf to have babies, she finds a quiet hole or cave called a "den." The newborn puppies live there with her for the first four to six weeks while they nurse. After that, it's time to bring in babysitters! Other wolves in the pack help the mother take care of the puppies. After seven or eight months, when the puppies are almost grown up, they start going on hunts with the rest of the pack. When a young wolf is one or two years old, it usually leaves the pack and tries to find a mate so it can start its own pack.

Wolves don't have houses exactly like you do, but each wolf pack does have its own home territory where it lives and hunts. If a wolf from a different pack tries to enter this territory, the pack will often chase it away! Think about it: you wouldn't want a stranger coming into your living room, would you?

Even though wolf packs don't like strange wolves in their territory, they usually don't worry about humans. For example, wolf packs generally ignore loggers who cut down trees and men who dig mines, even though those activities harm their habitat. For the most part, wolves just try to avoid people.

When it's time to eat, a wolf pack looks for deer, elk, caribou, antelope or other smaller wild animals to hunt. Sometimes, if they are very hungry and their territory is too small, wolves will attack sheep and cattle as well. That's why it is important for wolves to have plenty of room to roam and hunt. It might seem cruel when a wolf kills a deer, but wolves, like all wild carnivorous animals, kill prey only for food.

A long time ago, wolves lived everywhere in the United States, but not any more. Some farmers and other people who were worried about livestock hunted wolves until there were almost none left at all. Luckily, wolves did survive in Canada and the northern edge of Minnesota. Today, people who care about wolves have worked hard to bring them back into the wild parts of the United States. Since 1995, wolves have been successfully brought back into Yellowstone National Park and central Idaho, and they are being reintroduced into other states as well.

Why do wolves howl? A wolf may howl if it gets separated from its pack, but usually howling is a group activity. As one wolf starts to howl, the other members of the wolf pack join in. These howling choruses are more than just beautiful; they seem to help the wolves bond with other members of the pack. Howling may also be a kind of long-distance communication. The deep howling travels many miles and can be heard by other wolf packs far away.

—The Starfall staff.

*Visit www.starfall.com for
more information about wolves.*

About the Author

Margaret Hillert wrote her first poem when she was eight years old. At eighty-five she's still writing books and poems for children and adults all around the world.

Margaret knows what children like to read because she was a first-grade teacher for 34 years. She loves to visit her local library and read to children.

The Women's National Book Association honored Margaret in 1993 for writing wonderful children's books. But she says her BIGGEST reward has been teaching so many children how to read!

Word List - 64 Words

a	good	see(s)
and	happy	she
are	have	so
at	he	some
away	helps	something
babies	here	spot
baby	is	that
big	it	the
can	jump	this
cat	like	three
come	little	to
did	look	too
do	make	two
down	mother	wants
eat	no	what
father	not	where
find	now	will
for	oh	with
fun	one(s)	wolf
get	play	you
give	pretty	
go	run	